Something Else

For Carys — K.C.

Something Else

KATHRYN CAVE
ILLUSTRATED BY CHRIS RIDDELL

On a windy hill
alone
with nothing to be friends with
lived Something Else.

He knew that was what he was because everyone said so.

If he tried to sit with them
or walk with them
or join in their games,
they always said,

"Sorry. You're not like us.
You're something else.
You don't belong."

Something Else did his best
to be like the others.

He smiled and said "Hi!" like they did.

He painted pictures.

He played their games when they let him.

He brought his lunch in a paper bag like theirs.

It was no good.

He didn't look like them
or talk like them.

He didn't see the things they saw.

He didn't play the way they played.

As for his lunches...

"You don't belong here," they said.
"You're not like us. You're something else."

Something Else went home.
While he was getting ready for bed,
there was a knock on the door.

Something was standing on the doorstep.
"Hi there!" it said. "Great to meet you. Can I come in?"
"Excuse me?" said Something Else.

"You're welcome," said the creature.
It stuck out a paw, or maybe a flipper.

Something Else looked at the paw.
"I think you've come to the wrong place," he said.

The creature shook its head. "No, I haven't.
This place is perfect. Look!"

And before Something Else realized what was happening,
it walked right in...

and sat down on Something Else's supper.

"Do I know you?" asked Something Else, puzzled.
"Know me?" The creature laughed. "Of course you do!
Take a good look. Go on!"

Something Else looked.

He walked round the creature from front to back and back to front. He didn't know what to say, so he didn't say anything.

"Don't you see?" the creature cried. "I'm just like you! You're something else, and I'M ONE TOO!"
It stuck out its paw again and smiled.

Something Else was too surprised to smile back.
He didn't take the paw either.

"Like me?" he said. "You're not like me.
In fact, you're not like anything I've ever seen.
I'm sorry, but you're definitely not MY sort of something else."
He walked to the door and opened it. "Goodnight."

The creature put down its paw, slowly.
"Oh," it said.
It looked sadder and smaller.

It reminded Something Else of something,
but he couldn't think what.

While he was trying to remember, the creature left.

Then Something Else remembered.
"Wait!" he cried. "Don't go!"

He ran after the creature as fast as he could.
When he caught up, he grabbed its paw and held on tight.
"You're not like me, BUT I DON'T MIND.
You can stay with me if you'd like to."
And the creature did.

From then on, Something Else had Something to be friends with.

They smiled and said "Hi!"
to each other.

They painted pictures.

They played each other's games, or tried to.

They ate their lunches side by side.

They were different,
but they got along.

And when something turned up that really WAS weird looking, they didn't say he wasn't like them and he didn't belong there.

They moved right up
and made room for him, too.

Published in the United States of America in 1998
by **MONDO Publishing**
First published in the United Kingdom by Penguin Books Ltd, 1994

Text copyright © 1994 by Kathryn Cave
Illustrations copyright © 1994 by Chris Riddell

For information contact:
MONDO Publishing
One Plaza Road
Greenvale, New York 11548
Visit our web site at http://www.mondopub.com

Filmset in Bembo
Printed in Hong Kong
First Mondo Printing, November 1997
97 98 99 00 01 02 03 04   9 8 7 6 5 4 3 2 1

Library of Congress Cataloging-in-Publication Data
Cave, Kathryn.
    Something else / Kathryn Cave ; illustrated by Chris Riddell.
        p.   cm.
    Summary: A little creature is ostracized despite his attempts to fit in, but
his experiences enable him to be accepting of others' differences.
    ISBN 1-57255-563-7 (pbk. : alk. paper)
    [1. Individuality—Fiction. 2. Friendship—Fiction.] I. Riddell, Chris, ill.
II. Title.
PZ7.C29114So   1998
[E]—dc21
                                                                97-42258
                                                                    CIP
                                                                    AC